FIVE
TRUCKS
BRIAN FLOCA

A Richard Jackson Book
Atheneum Books for Young Readers
NEW YORK LONDON TORONTO SYDNEY NEW DELHI

For Dick Jackson

With thanks to Paul Cody *of American Airlines in
Boston, Massachusetts, for an up-close look at airport trucks
and their operations, and for reviewing an early draft of the book*

ATHENEUM BOOKS FOR YOUNG READERS
An imprint of Simon & Schuster Children's Publishing Division
1230 Avenue of the Americas, New York, New York 10020
Copyright © 1999 by Brian Floca
Originally published in 1999 by DK Publishing, Inc.
ATHENEUM BOOKS FOR YOUNG READERS
is a registered trademark of Simon & Schuster, Inc.
Atheneum logo is a trademark of Simon & Schuster, Inc.
For information about special discounts for bulk purchases, please contact
Simon & Schuster Special Sales at 1-866-506-1949 or business@simonandschuster.com.
The Simon & Schuster Speakers Bureau can bring authors to your live event.
For more information or to book an event, contact the Simon & Schuster Speakers Bureau
at 1-866-248-3049 or visit our website at www.simonspeakers.com.
The text of this book is set in New Caledonia LT.
The illustrations are rendered in watercolor, ink, and gouache.
Manufactured in China
0314 SCP
First Atheneum Books for Young Readers Edition June 2014
2 4 6 8 10 9 7 5 3 1
Library of Congress Cataloging-in-Publication Data
Floca, Brian.
Five trucks / Brian Floca ; illustrated by Brian Floca.
p.   cm
"A Richard Jackson Book."
"Originally published in 1999 by DK Publishing, Inc."—Copyright page.
Summary: Five different trucks do five different jobs to get an airplane ready for takeoff.
ISBN 978-1-4814-0593-5 (hardback)
[1. Trucks—Fiction. 2. Airports—Fiction.] I. Title.
PZ7.F6579Fi 2014
[E]—dc23
2013045225
ISBN 978-1-4814-0594-2 (eBook)

Five drivers
for
five trucks.

The first truck
is large and heavy.

The second truck
is small and quick.

The third truck

is long and straight.

The fourth truck

twists

and

turns.

The fifth truck
moves up . . .

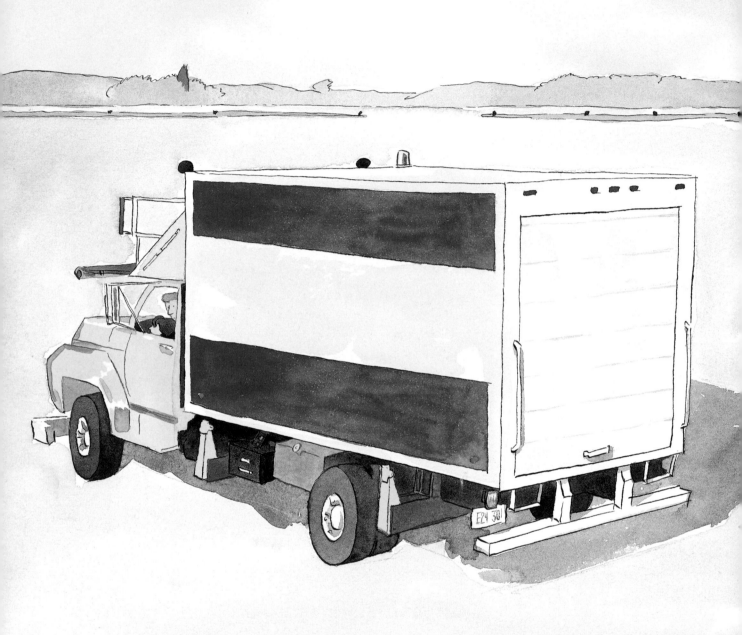

. . . and down.

Five trucks go
in one direction.

Food is unloaded from the fifth truck.

Catering truck

Luggage is unloaded from the fourth truck.

Tractor with baggage carts

The third truck
carries the luggage
up its back.

Baggage conveyor

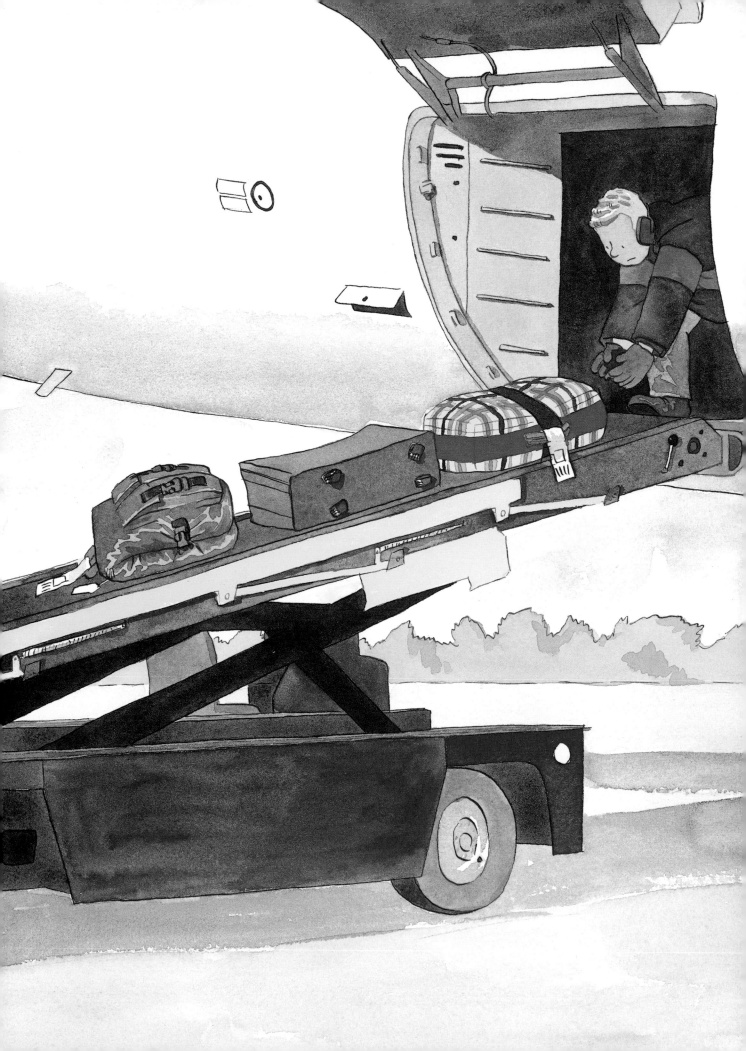

The mechanic takes
the second truck
to check the wheels.

A300   757   727

Tractor

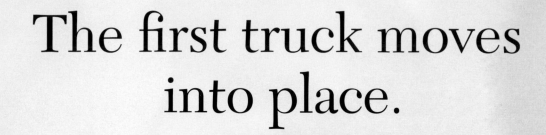

The first truck moves
into place.

When everything is ready,
it slowly pushes
forward . . .

Push-out tractor

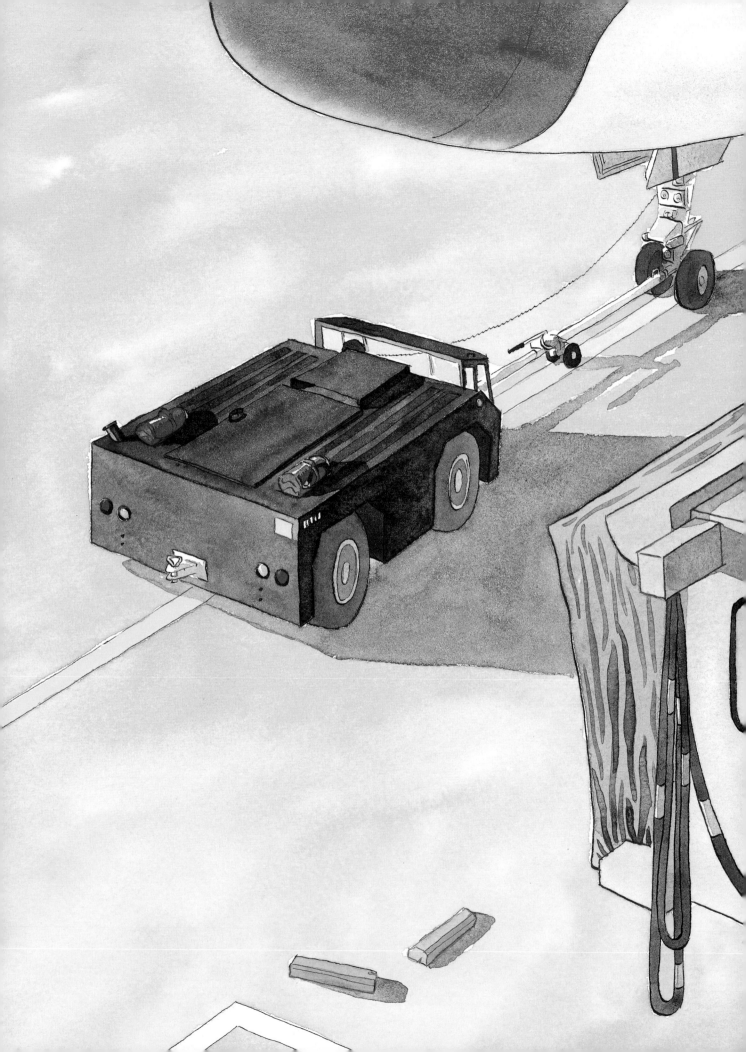

. . . one airplane.

The five drivers
of the five trucks watch
the airplane
speed down the runway . . .

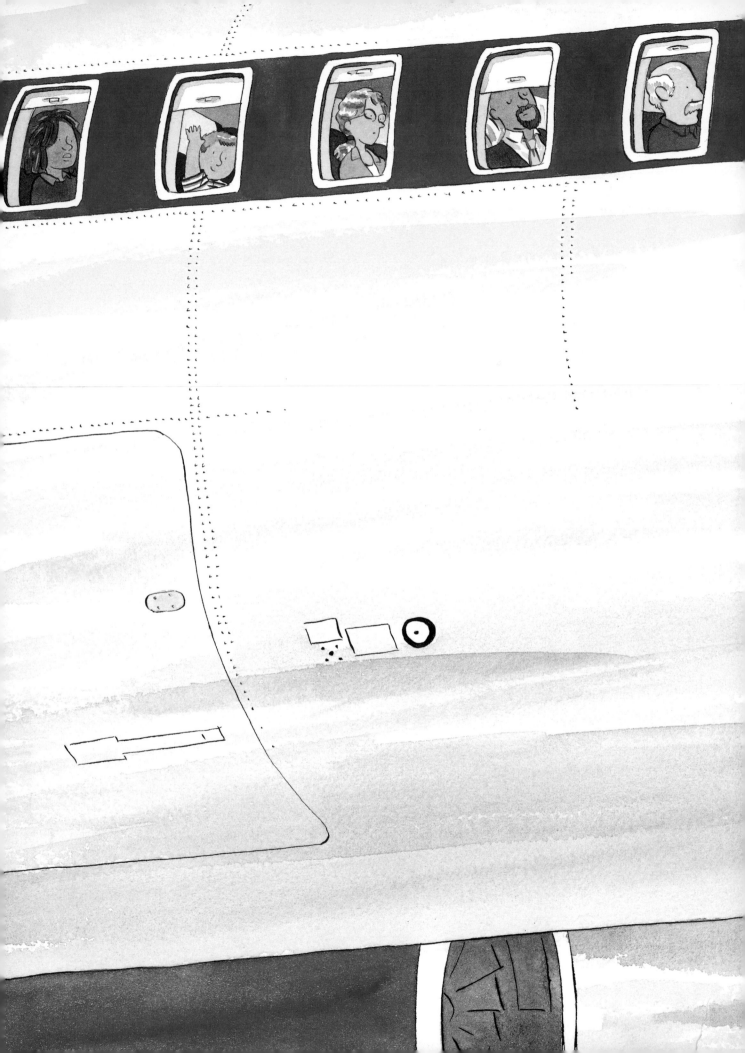

. . . faster and faster, until . . .

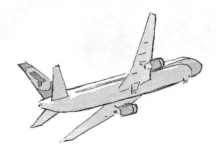

. . . takeoff!